PERSNICKITY

by
Stephen Cosgrove

Illustrated by
Robin James

A Serendipity™ Book

PRICE STERN SLOAN
Los Angeles

Dedicated to Teri Reasoner, though her house be filled with dragons, her socks are always clean.

Stephen

Once, in a land of magic mountains and dreams, there lived some mighty dragons in a shadowy valley called Olde Dragon Hollow. Here the dragons lived deep in a cave, carved from crystal coal. Here they hid from idle passersby who might have laughed, leered or jumped in fear of the mighty dragons that lived in Olde Dragon Hollow.

The dragons really couldn't scare anyone, for if you looked very carefully you would note that all the dragons wore wooly socks upon their feet to keep their toes warm on those cold, cold crystal cave nights. Nothing is very scary about a dragon who wears socks.

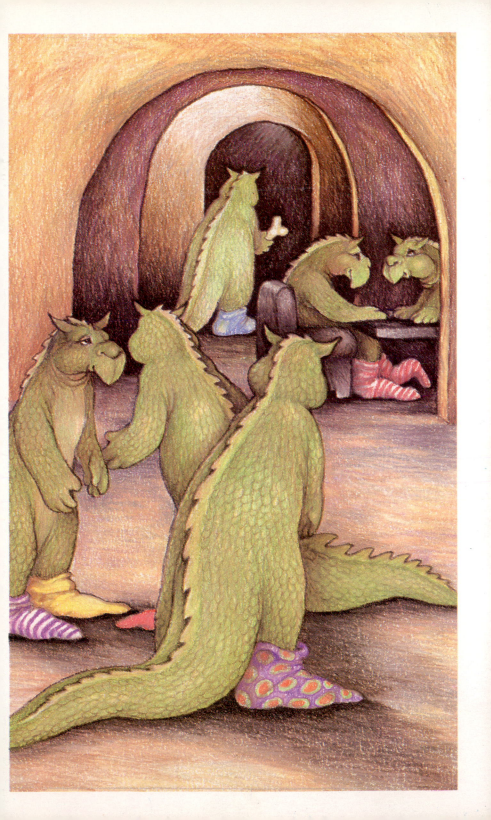

Now the dragons that lived in Olde Dragon Hollow were a sloppy lot. Sticks and bones from forgotten meals were strewn hither thither and non about the entrance to the cave. A bit of this and a bit of that was cast about. Why, they even left their dirty wooly socks draped across the rocks.

Olde Dragon Hollow was a mess and so were the mighty dragons that lived there. The dragons would sprawl about in the warm summer sun, dreaming of knights and days gone by. Occasionally, a dragon or two would burp a bit of oily smoke—and they didn't even say, "Excuse me!"

Olde Dragon Hollow was a sorry sight, a sorry sight indeed.

Not all of the dragons were sloppy, for one of the dragons was as clean as clean could be, and he was called Persnickity. His shiny green scales were combed and oiled to a shiny sheen. His face was scrubbed until it nearly glowed. Around his neck he wore a perfectly tied bow tie—always clean, always neat, always tied and on his feet he always wore a clean pair of checkered, ironed socks.

Persnickity spent most of his days trying to clean up after the other dragons. With an armful of dirty socks he would waddle to the stream to wash them all as the other dragons ate another messy meal of grease, glop and bones.

Now it wasn't that the other dragons didn't appreciate the things that Persnickity did, it was just that they didn't care if things were messy or not and, if they were to choose, they preferred messy more.

One day the little pristine dragon became very angry. "That's it!" he cried as he threw down a pile of rubbish, "I'll wash not another sock. I will pick up nary another bone! If all of you wish to act like pigs then you should live like them too!"

"Gee, thanks Persnickity," they all shouted in glee as they began throwing food at one another. "We're just as happy dirty as you are clean."

"Well!" Persnickity exclaimed, "If that's the way you feel, then I am moving far away—far away indeed!"

The other dragons thought about it a moment or two and then chorused, "okay" and went back to their food fight.

Persnickity rushed into the cave and carefully packed all of his belongings. He packed his ties, several handkerchiefs with his initials stitched on the side, all of his checkered stockings, his toothbrush and his favorite bar of soap.

After all was packed, he nattily washed his hands and face, put on a clean pair of socks, picked up his bag and carefully stepped around the sleeping dragons. The wind whispered cleanly through the trees as Persnickity walked away from Olde Dragon Hollow and into the Valley of Streams and Dreams.

"Oh, what a delightful valley," he shouted in glee as he walked beside the crystal waters of the stream. "It's all so neat and clean. Oh, and it is so perfect."

Persnickity walked and walked, looking at all the perfection around him. He stopped to smell some bright red roses, but as he touched the stem of the rose, a thorn pricked his finger. "Hmm," he thought, "it's pretty perfect but not perfect enough. When I build my perfect little house I shall pluck all the thorns from those roses and then they'll be perfect too."

Persnickity picked a perfect spot on a perfect knoll to build his perfect house. He only used perfect stones and sticks from which to build his perfect little house. When he was done the house was perfectly square with perfect little windows and a perfect little door.

He stood back to examine all the perfection that he had perfected when he backed into a thorn on one of the pesky roses. "Ouch," he cried. "Well, little flowers now it's your turn." And for the rest of the day he picked and plucked all the nasty thorns from the bright red roses that grew about his little stone cottage.

"There," he said as he dusted his hands carefully clean, "now I have perfect flowers around my perfect house in a perfect part of the world." Then he walked inside to begin living his perfect life.

But all was not perfect, for Persnickity had no one to admire all his perfection. He moped about the meadow and finally came up with a marvelous plan. "I shall throw a perfect party. I'll invite all the dragons from Olde Dragon Hollow and then they shall see how perfect a clean life can be."

He dashed inside and neatly wrote an invitation to all the dragons. Then he rushed about making perfect sandwiches and a perfect cake for the perfect party. When all was done and set neatly on the table, he slipped into his bed with its crisply ironed sheets and tightly tucked blankets and fell into a perfect sleep and dreamed of clean and folded things.

The next day, like a rumbling summer storm, all the dragons rambled into the Valley of Streams and Dreams. They rollicked and frolicked and had just a delightful time throwing food and draping their socks all over the house. They wrestled on the floor, ate all the food or threw it and burped in great gales of laughter. All in all the dragons had a perfect party.

All of them, that is, except Persnickity, who rushed about picking up all that they threw down. "Wipe your feet! Use a napkin! Don't touch! Don't look! Just don't!" Persnickity shouted as he rushed from one end of the house to the other and cleaned all the spills that were made.

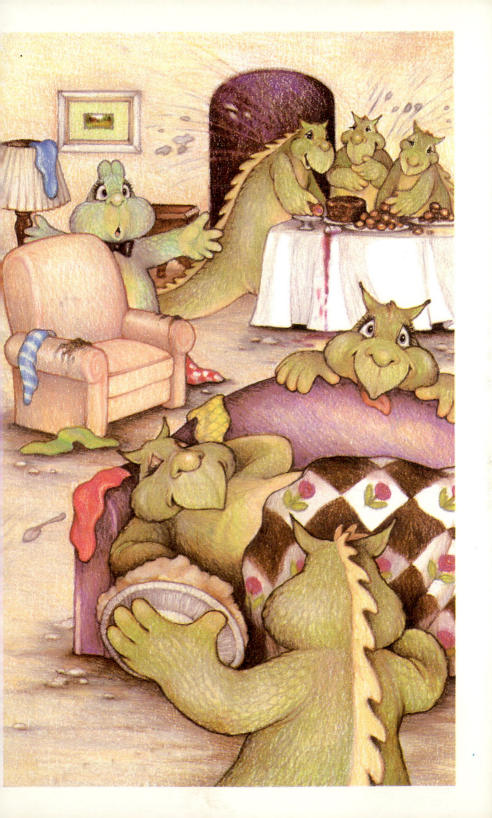

The dragons tore up the inside of the house and then rushed outside. Now, dragons love to eat rosebuds but usually don't because of the thorns. Persnickity's roses had no thorns and they were able to pick and eat the blossoms—and the roses they didn't eat they threw about. Finally, Persnickity could stand no more and he stood in the door and roared, "Stop! You have ruined my perfect party!"

The dragons froze like messy statues and then one of them spoke, "No, I don't think so. The party was perfect, in part, because we had fun!"

"But," stammered Persnickity, "my perfect house is a shambles and you have picked all the perfect roses, too!"

"Yeah," said the dragon with a dumb smile on his face, "we never could pick the bright red roses before because of the thorns but you have made them perfect." With that he picked the final rose and popped it into his mouth and ate it.

Now that the party was over, the dragons put back on their oddly matched, soiled socks and rolled like a dust storm back to their home in Olde Dragon Hollow. They left behind a monstrous mess. Everywhere Persnickity looked there was no perfection. His bed was tossed and turned, there was jam and jelly stuck to the ceiling—why, there was even a dirty sock draped about the leftover cake. With grim resolve never to have a perfect party again, Persnickity began to clean up the mess.

He cleaned and cleaned all through the night, buffing and shining everything bright. Then, at first morning's light, he stepped outside and looked at his once again perfect house.

But all was not perfect, for the roses that had grown so perfectly were torn and trampled down. Persnickity sat down with a thump and a puff of dust. With a small, trickling tear sliding down his cheek, he picked up a tattered rose.

He stifled a sob as he looked and looked at the tattered rose. But the more he thought about the party, the more he found perfection in all the mess. He began to giggle as he realized that perfection is only perfection if you have something to compare it to. What better to compare to a perfect house than the dragon's perfect mess.

He laughed and laughed as he swept up the flowers, "The party was perfect and in a dusty, dirty sort of way—those dragons are sort of perfect. The roses would have lived if I had only left on the thorns." With that he dashed about his garden and carefully taped a thorn onto every bush.

From that day forward Persnickity threw a party once a year and all the dragons came just as messy as could be. They ate and threw the food. They jumped upon the bed. But they never ate the roses, the roses bright, bright red. For the stem of every rose was gaily adorned with imperfect thorns that made each flower even more perfect.

PERFECTLY PERFECT IS GOOD
OR SO THE STORY GOES
BUT NATURE LEFT ALL ON HER OWN
WILL MAKE A PERFECT ROSE

Serendipity™ Books

Written by Stephen Cosgrove
Illustrated by Robin James

Enjoy all the delightful books in the Serendipity Series:

BANGALEE*	LEO THE LOP TAIL TWO*
BUTTERMILK	LEO THE LOP TAIL THREE*
BUTTERMILK BEAR	LITTLE MOUSE ON THE PRAIRIE*
CAP'N SMUDGE*	MAUI-MAUI*
CATUNDRA*	MEMILY
CRABBY GABBY	MING LING*
CREOLE*	MINIKIN
CRICKLE-CRACK	MISTY MORGAN
DRAGOLIN	MORGAN AND ME*
THE DREAM TREE*	MORGAN AND YEW*
FANNY	MORGAN MINE*
FEATHER FIN*	MORGAN MORNING*
FLUTTERBY*	THE MUFFIN MUNCHER*
FLUTTERBY FLY	MUMKIN
GABBY*	NITTER PITTER
GLITTERBY BABY	PISH POSH
THE GNOME FROM NOME*	RAZ-MA-TAZ*
GRAMPA-LOP*	SERENDIPITY*
HUCKLEBUG*	SHIMMEREE*
IN SEARCH OF THE SAVEOPOTOMAS*	SNAFFLES*
JAKE O'SHAWNASEY*	SQUEAKERS
JINGLE BEAR	TEE-TEE
KARTUSCH*	TRAFALGAR TRUE*
KIYOMI	TRAPPER*
LEO THE LOP*	WHEEDLE ON THE NEEDLE*

The above books, and many others, can be bought wherever books
are sold, or may be ordered directly from the publisher.

PRICE STERN SLOAN

360 North La Cienega Boulevard, Los Angeles, California 90048